This Little Tiger book belongs to:

_____

_____

_____

For Betty, who sorts everybody out (especially Little Lenny!) ~ S S

For Matt Upsher, his family, his friends and all those he inspired ~ C P

LITTLE TIGER PRESS
1 The Coda Centre,
189 Munster Road, London SW6 6AW
www.littletiger.co.uk

First published in Great Britain 2011
This edition published 2012
Text copyright © Steve Smallman 2011
Illustrations copyright © Caroline Pedler 2011
Steve Smallman and Caroline Pedler have asserted their rights
to be identified as the author and illustrator of this work
under the Copyright, Designs and Patents Act, 1988
A CIP catalogue record for this book
is available from the British Library
All rights reserved

ISBN 978-1-84895-226-3
LTP/1900/0883/0314
Printed in China
10 9 8 7 6 5 4 3 2

Who's Afraid of the Big Bad Bunny?

Steve Smallman   Caroline Pedler

LITTLE TIGER PRESS
London

"I'm hungry!" said little Lenny bunny.
"I'm **very** hungry!" said slightly bigger
Benny bunny.

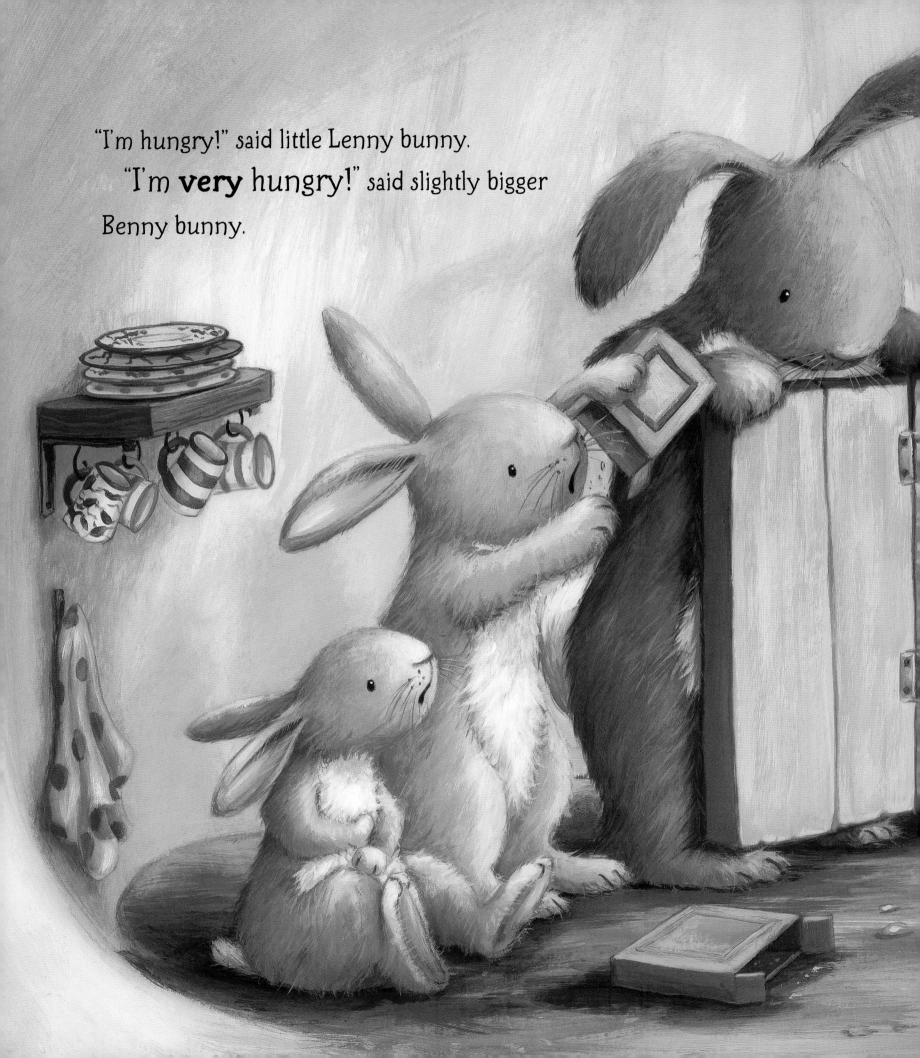

"I'm **very**, **very** hungry!"
said much bigger Barney bunny.

"Well, someone had better go to
the vegetable patch and get some
carrots then because there are none left!"
said itty bitty Betty bunny.

"I'll go!" said little Lenny. And off he went.

Little Lenny bunny had just pulled up
one big, juicy carrot when
out jumped...

a
Big
Bad
Bully
Bunny!

He **pushed** poor Lenny on to his little bunny bottom and **snatched** the carrot.

"You can't have this carrot!" he shouted.

"Why not?" squeaked little Lenny.

"Because you're really, really **stupid!**" bellowed the Big Bad Bully Bunny.

"And if you tell anyone that I took your carrot, I'll squash you flat!"

Poor Lenny bunny went back to his burrow empty-handed.

"Why didn't you bring us any carrots?" asked his brothers and sister.

"Because I'm too stupid," said little Lenny, in a very small voice.

"No you're not! Who told you that?" they asked.

But little Lenny bunny
wouldn't tell.

"Don't worry!" said slightly
bigger Benny bunny. "I'll get
us some carrots!"
And off he went.

Benny bunny had just pulled up
two juicy looking carrots
when...
out jumped the **Big Bad Bully Bunny.**

He **pushed** over poor Benny bunny and **snatched** the carrots.

"You can't have these carrots!"

he shouted.

"Why not?" gasped Benny bunny.

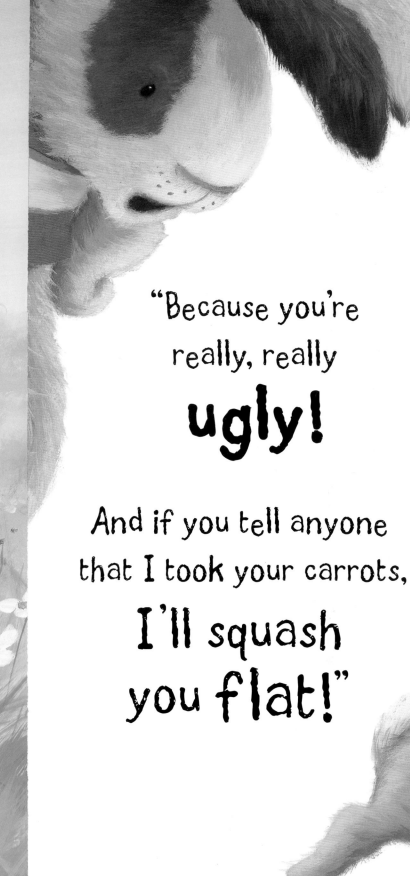

"Because you're really, really **ugly!**

And if you tell anyone that I took your carrots, **I'll squash you flat!**"

Poor Benny bunny went back home empty-handed.

"Why didn't **you** bring us any carrots?" asked Barney and Betty.

"Because I'm too ugly," said Benny bunny, in a very small voice.

"No you're not! Who told you that?" they asked.

But Benny bunny wouldn't tell.

"Don't worry!" said much bigger Barney bunny. "I'll get us some carrots!"

And off he went.

Barney bunny had just
pulled up three juicy looking
carrots when ...

out jumped the
**Big
Bad
Bully
Bunny.**

"You can't have these carrots!" he shouted.

"W... w... why not?" stuttered Barney bunny.

"Because you're really, really fat and **wobbly!** And if you tell anyone that I took your carrots, I'll squash you flat!"

Poor Barney bunny went back home empty-handed.

"Why didn't **you** bring us any carrots **either**?" cried Betty.

"Because I'm too fat and wobbly," sniffed Barney bunny, in a very small voice.

"No you're not! Who told you that?" she asked.

But Barney bunny wouldn't tell.

"This is just silly!" shouted itty bitty Betty bunny.

"Barney, you are **not** fat or wobbly!

Benny, you're **not** ugly!

And you are **not** stupid, Lenny."

"Now. Who's been saying these nasty things to you?"

"The Big Bad Bully Bunny," said Lenny, Benny and Barney bunny in three very small voices.

"Well, why didn't you say something?" said Betty. "Together we can sort out any bad bully!"

Itty bitty Betty bunny took all of
her brothers to the vegetable patch to pick
some carrots. Lenny, Benny and
Barney bunny were very
nervous but they quickly pulled up...

a
great
big
pile of
carrots.

Out jumped...

...the Big **Bad** **Bully** Bunny!

"You can't have these carrots!"

he shouted.

"Why not?"

asked Betty bunny.

"Because you're just a stupid, ugly, big, fat, **wobbly girl!**"

bellowed the Big Bad Bully Bunny.

"No I'm not,"
said the little rabbit.
"**You** are!"

"N... no I'm not!"
cried the Big Bad Bully Bunny.
"Just give me
those carrots...
now!"

Then Betty, Lenny, Benny and Barney
bunny all shouted

"NO!"

The Big Bad Bully Bunny was so

surprised that he fell on to his big,

bully bunny
bottom
with a great big bump!

"But I'm hungry!" wailed the Bad Bully Bunny, who suddenly didn't feel so big any more. "**Give me some carrots!**" he whined. "**Now!**"

Betty whispered something to Lenny, Benny and Barney. And they all heaved and pushed until they tipped over the wheelbarrow full of carrots…

...and squashed him
flat!

And he never **ever** bullied bunnies again.

More fabulously funny books from Little Tiger Press!

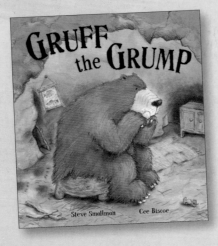

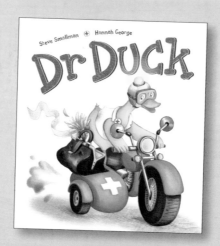

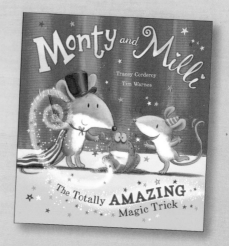

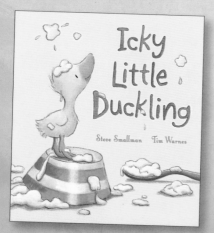

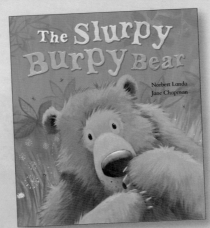

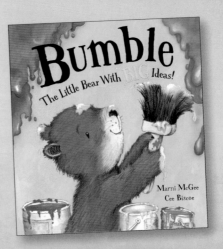

For information regarding any of the above titles or
for our catalogue, please contact us:
Little Tiger Press, 1 The Coda Centre,
189 Munster Road, London SW6 6AW
Tel: 020 7385 6333 • Fax: 020 7385 7333
E-mail: contact@littletiger.co.uk
www.littletiger.co.uk